Racing Danger

by Minnie Timenti
illustrated by Tom McNeely

 HOUGHTON MIFFLIN · BOSTON

1855

In 1855, Mary Ann Patten was eighteen years old. She had been married for two years. Her husband, Joshua Patten, was a young sea captain. He commanded the clipper ship *Neptune's Car.*

Clippers were the fastest sailing ships in the world at that time. Yet ocean voyages could last months. Captains sometimes brought their families on board, so Mary joined her husband on the *Neptune's Car.*

On board the ship, Mary had many duties. She treated sick or injured sailors. She helped with the cooking. She also spent a lot of time learning how the ship worked.

3

Joshua gave Mary lessons in navigating. She learned how to use instruments and charts to guide a ship. She learned to make day-by-day entries in the logbook.

Neptune's Car went from New York to San Fransisco in 101 days. Mary learned many skills during that time. She would need those skills on her next voyage.

Clipper ships often raced against one another. Shipping companies used the races to advertise their business.

On July 1, 1856, *Neptune's Car,* under the command of Captain Patten, set sail from New York for San Francisco. Mary was on board. The ship would race against two others. Which ship would be first to cover fifteen thousand miles of ocean?

Neptune's Car sailed south swiftly. But before long Captain Patten had a big problem. The first mate, a man named Keeler, seemed to want to slow down the ship. He fell asleep while on duty. He disobeyed orders.

Captain Patten could not permit such behavior. He had Keeler locked up below deck, and Patten took on the first mate's tasks himself.

The ship sailed farther south. The sky and the sea turned gray. Rolling waves rose to frightening heights. Strong winds blew. The ship was nearing Cape Horn, the tip of South America. The seas here were the worst in the world, known for fierce storms, ice floes, and shipwrecks.

Freezing winds blasted the *Neptune's Car*. Icy waves washed over the deck. Captain Patten used ropes to tie himself to the rail so that he would not be swept overboard. Except for a few short naps, he always seemed to be awake. Day and night, Patten guided his ship through the perilous seas. But after two weeks, his body gave out.

Captain Patten had a high fever. He became
blind. He cried out, but his words made no
sense. Filled with worry, Mary checked medical
books. She tried to treat her husband's illness,
but she was unable to cure him.

The first mate usually took over when a captain was ill. But Keeler was locked up, and the second mate didn't know how to navigate a clipper ship. Something had to be done quickly to make sure the ship survived the journey.

Mary Ann Patten knew what she had to do. She took command of *Neptune's Car*. Keeler tried to convince the sailors to work against her. He told them that the ship would go down if it were led by a woman.

Mary ordered the crew to gather on deck. She told the men that she could guide the ship to San Francisco, but only if they obeyed her. The men listened to the steady voice of their captain's wife. She seemed so brave and so sure of herself, they all agreed to work with her.

Mary studied the charts and maps. She made measurements. She figured out where the ship was and where it had to go.

Neptune's Car plunged through high waves. Powerful snowstorms raged. Mary plotted the course of the ship and cared for her husband. She was often on deck. And when the winds screamed, she shouted her orders through a horn. She barely slept.